dance!

ELISHA COOPER

 Greenwillow Books, *An Imprint of* HarperCollins*Publishers*

Rehearsal starts early. Dancers arrive at the studio wearing comfortable clothes.

They peel off layers of sweatpants, sweaters, and socks and

toss them on chairs and in corners. Then they stretch. One dancer groans.

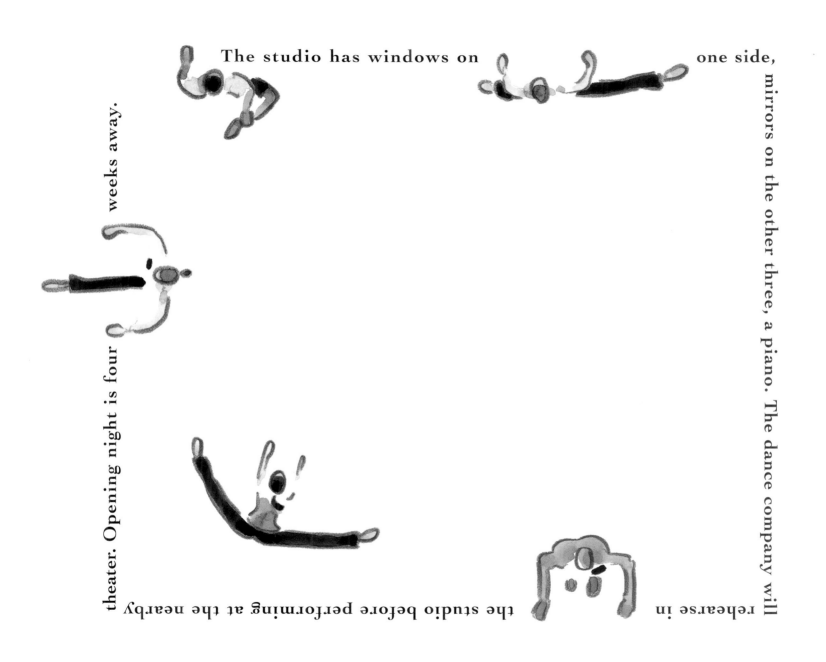

The studio has windows on one side, mirrors on the other three, a piano. The dance company will rehearse in the studio before performing at the nearby theater. Opening night is four weeks away.

The dancers warm up at the barre and wait for the choreographer.

Their feet squeak on the floor, and it sounds as if they are scrubbing it clean.

The choreographer bursts through
the studio door. He greets. He kisses.

He gathers the company and tells them his ideas for
the dance. He demonstrates, and the dancers follow,
imitating his big moves with little moves of their own.

He talks the whole time:
EVERY! WORD!
HE! SAYS! HAS! AN!
EXCLAMATION! POINT!

The choreographer makes up
some of the dance as he goes.

The next day the dancers practice steps on their own. They look at their feet in the mirror as they move. The choreographer stands to the side and claps as he counts: "AND ONE AND TWO AND JUMP AND YES!" He moves a dancer's leg to the correct position as if he were molding clay.

Another dancer suggests changes—using his body in a conversation without words. When the dancers are frustrated, the choreographer stops and tells a joke. The dancers rehearse until their arms and legs remember the steps.

A pianist plays with the dancers, his notes tripping after them as they move across the floor. The dancers play with the music, reaching out as if to catch the notes as they rise and fall around the studio.

A clarinetist and a drummer come to the studio to accompany
the dancers. Drumbeats run through the floor and up the dancers'
legs and into their chests. Rhythm and movement work in unison.

When the music stops, all that can be heard is the dancers'
breathing. Panting, they lie in a puddle on the floor and suck
bottles of water. Hair sticks to foreheads. The tails of shirts
that had been tied into knots come undone. The dancers towel
sweat and talk about which parts of their bodies ache.

Before showering, a woman walks
on a man's back to make it feel better.

After rehearsal the dancers walk from the studio to
a market to buy food for dinner. They choose mounds
of vegetables and fruit, pasta and meat, chocolate.

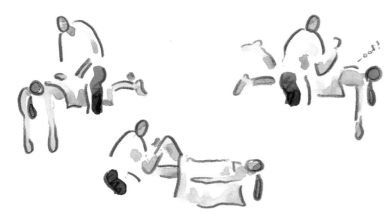

A dancer visits a masseur with big hands, who prods and pokes the dancer's back, neck, thighs, calves, arms, and feet—even her toes.

A dancer goes home and wraps a bag of ice around her ankle. Calluses and blisters cover her feet, and her feet aren't pretty.

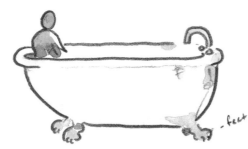

Another dancer takes a hot bath.

In the following days the dancers repeat steps over and over again.
One dancer leaps into the air, and it takes seconds for her to land.

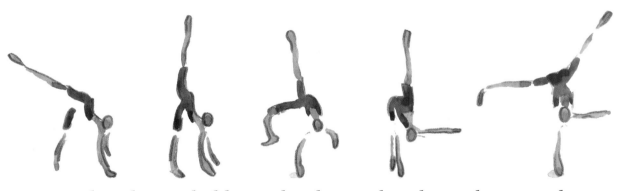

Another dancer holds up the sky, pushes down the ground.
He lifts himself with one hand, and his back muscles ripple.

A dancer turns and cradles the air between his arms.
When he dances lightly, it takes the most strength of all.

One dancer is so flexible, she can touch the top of her head with both big toes. Her spine curves, and she touches her nose to her belly button.

A dancer dances with his hands, watching them as if they weren't his, as if he were surprised to find five fingers at the end of each arm.

A dancer twists, and sometimes it's hard to tell which body part is attached to which part of the body. She becomes letters in the alphabet.

In the last weeks dancers practice difficult lifts and jumps.

A man and a woman dance a duet.

He thrusts her into the air

as his feet shuffle for balance.

She walks up the front of his body.

He tosses her over his shoulder like a rug.

Two bodies work as one.

The dance is almost ready.

The dance company moves to the theater. The box office sits between the front doors. Above the box office are clean and bright white lights and the marquee on which a theater worker hangs black letters.

Backstage there are mops, fans, boxes, trash cans, stools, rags, the door to the dressing room, the rope for the red curtain, a theater worker climbing a ladder to adjust the lights. Duct tape holds everything together.

The costume designer works with
the choreographer to design costumes.

A dancer tries one on, and the designer
circles her with a mouthful of pins.

A dancer's feet poke out
from under her dress.

When her dress fits,

the dancer leaps into the air,

testing it until it feels like a second skin.

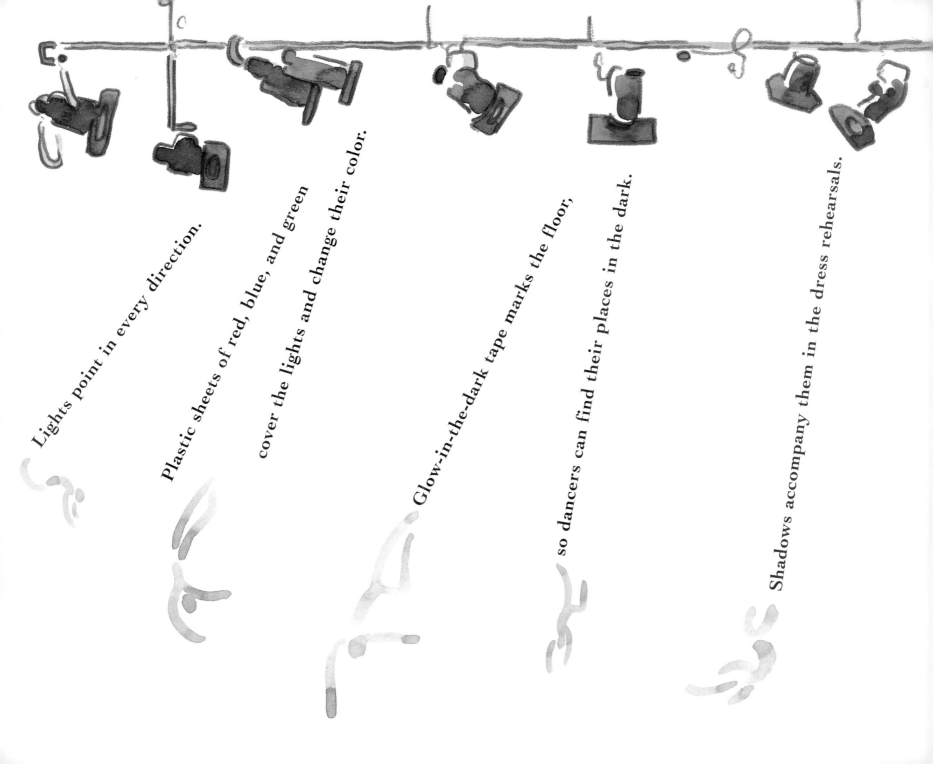

Lights point in every direction.

Plastic sheets of red, blue, and green cover the lights and change their color.

Glow-in-the-dark tape marks the floor, so dancers can find their places in the dark.

Shadows accompany them in the dress rehearsals.

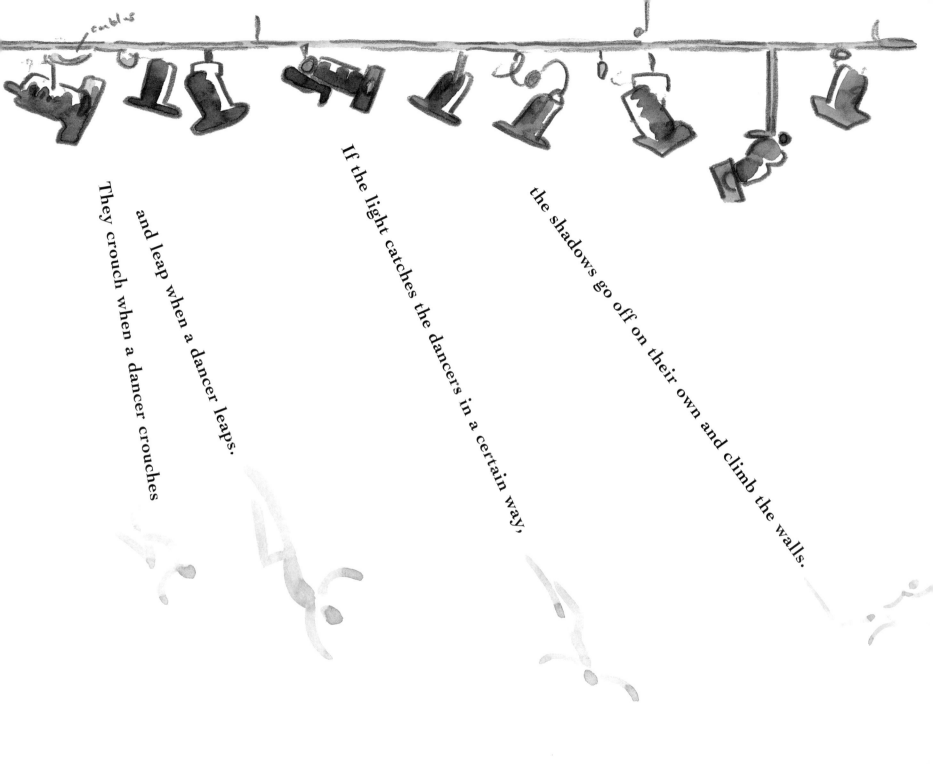

cables

They crouch when a dancer crouches

and leap when a dancer leaps.

If the light catches the dancers in a certain way,

the shadows go off on their own and climb the walls.

After the last dress rehearsal the dancers meet with the choreographer. He holds a pad of paper and gives final notes and suggestions. The dancers sprawl on the floor and listen—there is motion even in their stillness.

At the end of the meeting the dancers practice their bows. After that they play and galumph. They pretend they are storks looking for fish, tortoises returning to sea, or bears running downhill. Then they go home and rest.

The dance company orders tickets and programs,

posters for subways and buses,

advertisements for newspapers and magazines.

In the program the dancers mention the schools they went to, people who helped them.

They write about themselves in the third person: "She wishes to thank her dog."

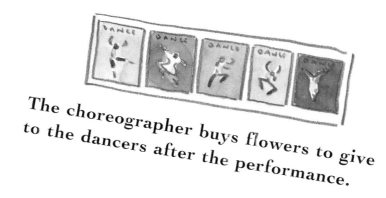

The choreographer buys flowers to give to the dancers after the performance.

Opening night.

A crowd forms outside the theater, bustling for tickets. The dancers
gather backstage. They can hear the buzz of the audience finding
seats, the beating of their own hearts. They hug.
The choreographer tells them they are wonderful.
The lights go down.

The curtain goes up.

For my cleats

Dance!
Copyright © 2001 by Elisha Cooper
All rights reserved.
Printed in Singapore by Tien Wah Press.
www.harperchildrens.com

Watercolors and pencil were used to prepare the full-color art.
The text type is Cochin Bold.

Library of Congress Cataloging-in-Publication Data
Cooper, Elisha.
Dance! / by Elisha Cooper.
p.   cm.
"Greenwillow Books."
ISBN 0-06-029418-3 (trade). ISBN 0-06-029419-1 (lib. bdg.)
1. Dance—Juvenile literature. [1. Dance. 2. Dancers.] I. Title.
GV1596.5 C67 2001   793.8-dc21 00-041102

1   2   3   4   5   6   7   8   9   10   First Edition

DATE DUE